Super Ben's Dirty Hands:
A Book About Healthy Habits

by Shelley Marshall   Illustrated by Ben Mahan

Super Ben and Molly the Great need to fight germs. They do not want to get sick. What can they do? **Let's read!**

Enslow Elementary
an imprint of
Enslow Publishers, Inc.
40 Industrial Road
Box 398
Berkeley Heights, NJ 07922
USA

http://www.enslow.com

Molly and Ben are at the park.

"Look!" Molly calls.

"Don't worry, little guy," says Ben. "We will save you!"

Ben turns the turtle over. The shell is wet and cold.

Thank you!

That bird looks lost!

"I will help!" Ben says.

Ben puts the nest back in the tree. It is dry and hard.

7

"Let's race!" says Molly.

Molly and Ben roll down the hill. Who won?

"This work makes me hungry," says Ben.

"Me, too," says Molly. "Let's eat!"

"Yum!" says Ben.

"Wait!" says Molly. "Look at your hands."

"They must be full of germs," says Molly.

"Think about all the things we touched."

"You are right," says Ben. "Let's wash our hands.
We do not want to be super sick heroes."

"Germs, germs, go away," Ben sings.

"And DO NOT come back another day!" says Molly.

Uh-oh. Ben's nose has a tickle. Here comes a big sneeze. *Ah-ha-ha-chooo!*

"Good job, Ben!" says Molly.

"You covered your sneeze with your arm!"

"Ha, ha, germs!" Ben says. "You will not get me!"

Read More About Healthy Habits

Books

McMahon, Kara. *Happy Healthy Monsters: Squeaky Clean.* New York: Random House, 2006.

Verdick, Elizabeth. *Germs Are Not For Sharing.* Minneapolis, MN: Free Spirit Publishing, 2006.

Web Site

Kids Next Door

www.hud.gov/kids/people.html

Enslow Elementary, an imprint of Enslow Publishers, Inc.

Enslow Elementary® is a registered trademark of Enslow Publishers, Inc.

Copyright © 2010 by Enslow Publishers, Inc.

Library of Congress Cataloging-in-Publication Data
Marshall, Shelley, 1968-
  Super Ben's dirty hands : a book about healthy habits / Shelley Marshall.
    p. cm. — (Character education with Super Ben and Molly the Great)
  ISBN 978-0-7660-3513-3
  1. Hygiene—Juvenile literature. 2. Health—Juvenile literature. I. Title.
  RA777.M268 2010
  613—dc22
                    2009000496

ISBN-13: 978-0-7660-3738-0 (paperback edition)

Printed in the United States of America

112009 Lake Book Manufacturing, Inc., Melrose Park, IL

10 9 8 7 6 5 4 3 2 1

To Our Readers: We have done our best to make sure all Internet Addresses in this book were active and appropriate when we went to press. However, the author and the publisher have no control and assume no liability for the material available on those Internet sites or on other Web sites they may link to. Any comments or suggestions can be sent by e-mail to comments@enslow.com or to the address on the back cover.

♻ Enslow Publishers, Inc. is committed to printing our books on recycled paper. The paper in every book contains 10% to 30% post-consumer waste (PCW). The cover board on the outside of every book contains 100% PCW. Our goal is to do our part to help young people and the environment too!